WAR AND PEACE

SECOND EPILOGUE

By Leo Tolstoy

Double 9
BOOKS

War and Peace
SECOND EPILOGUE
By Leo Tolstoy

ISBN: 978-93-94973-21-3

Published by

DOUBLE 9 BOOKS

2/13-B, Ansari Road
Daryaganj, New Delhi - 110002
info@double9books.com
www.double9books.com
Tel. 011-40042856

Printed in India.

About the Author

Leo Tolstoy was a Russian creator known for his books War and Peace which is viewed as the best book of pragmatist fiction. Tolstoy is additionally viewed as world's best author by quite a few people. Additionally an ethical scholar and a social reformer, Tolstoy had extreme moralistic points of view. In later life, he turned into an intense Christian rebel and anarcho-conservative.

Leo Tolstoy Born in Yasnaya Polyana on September 9, 1828, He had a place with a notable honorable Russian family. He was the fourth among five offspring of Count Nikolai Ilyich Tolstoy and Countess Mariya Tolstaya, both of whom kicked the bucket passing on their youngsters to be raised by family members.

In 1844, Tolstoy was acknowledged into Kazan University. Incapable to graduate past the subsequent year, Tolstoy got back to Yasnava Polyana and afterward invested energy going among Moscow and St. Petersburg. With some functioning information on a few dialects, he turned into a multilingual. Yet again the recently observed youth pulled in Tolstoy towards drinking, visiting massage parlors and most betting which left him in weighty obligation and anguish however Tolstoy before long acknowledged he was carrying on with a brutish life and endeavored college tests with the expectation that he would acquire a situation with the public authority, yet finished yet up in Caucuses serving in the military continuing in the strides of his senior sibling.

In Year 1862, Leo Tolstoy wedded Sophia Andreevna Behrs, generally called Sonya, who was 16 years more youthful than him. The couple had thirteen youngsters, of which, five passed on at an early age. Sonya went about as Tolstoy's secretary, editor and monetary chief while he made two out of his most prominent works. Their initial wedded life was loaded up with happiness.

He started composing his show-stopper, War and Peace in 1862. The six volumes of the work were distributed somewhere in the range of 1863 and 1869. With 580 characters got from history and others made by Tolstoy, this extraordinary novel takes on investigating the hypothesis of history and the irrelevance of noted figures like Alexander and Napoleon. Anna Karenina, Tolstoy's next epic was begun in 1873 and distributed totally in 1878.

Contents

SECOND EPILOGUE

CHAPTER I

H istory is the life of nations and of humanity. To seize and put into words, to describe directly the life of humanity or even of a single nation, appears impossible.

The ancient historians all employed one and the same method to describe and seize the apparently elusive—the life of a people. They described the activity of individuals who ruled the people, and regarded the activity of those men as representing the activity of the whole nation.

The question: how did individuals make nations act as they wished and by what was the will of these individuals themselves guided? the ancients met by recognizing a divinity which subjected the nations to the will of a chosen man, and guided the will of that chosen man so as to accomplish ends that were predestined.

For the ancients these questions were solved by a belief in the direct participation of the Deity in human affairs.

Modern history, in theory, rejects both these principles.

It would seem that having rejected the belief of the ancients in man's subjection to the Deity and in a predetermined aim toward which nations are led, modern history should study not the manifestations of power but the causes that produce it. But modern history has not done this. Having in theory rejected the view held by the ancients, it still follows them in practice.

Instead of men endowed with divine authority and directly guided by the will of God, modern history has given us either heroes endowed with extraordinary, superhuman capacities, or simply men of very various kinds, from monarchs to journalists, who lead the masses. Instead of the former divinely appointed aims of the Jewish, Greek, or Roman nations, which ancient historians regarded as representing the progress of humanity, modern history has postulated its own aims—the welfare of the French, German, or English people, or, in its highest abstraction, the welfare and civilization of humanity in general, by which is usually meant that of the peoples occupying a small northwesterly portion of a large continent.

Modern history has rejected the beliefs of the ancients without replacing them by a new conception, and the logic of the situation has obliged the historians, after they had apparently rejected the divine authority of the kings and the "fate" of the ancients, to reach the same conclusion by another road, that is, to recognize (1) nations guided by individual men, and (2) the existence of a known aim to which these nations and humanity at large are tending.

At the basis of the works of all the modern historians from Gibbon to Buckle, despite their seeming disagreements and the apparent novelty of their outlooks, lie those two old, unavoidable assumptions.

In the first place the historian describes the activity of individuals who in his opinion have directed humanity (one historian considers only monarchs, generals, and ministers as being such men, while another includes also orators, learned men, reformers, philosophers, and poets). Secondly, it is assumed that the goal toward which humanity is being led is known to the historians: to one of them this goal is the greatness of the Roman, Spanish, or French realm; to another it is liberty, equality, and a certain kind of civilization of a small corner of the world called Europe.

In 1789 a ferment arises in Paris; it grows, spreads, and is expressed by a movement of peoples from west to east. Several times it moves eastward and collides with a countermovement from the east westward. In 1812 it reaches its extreme limit, Moscow, and then, with remarkable symmetry, a countermovement occurs from east to west, attracting to it, as the first movement had done, the nations of middle Europe. The counter movement reaches the starting point of the first movement in the west—Paris—and subsides.

During that twenty-year period an immense number of fields were left untilled, houses were burned, trade changed its direction, millions of men migrated, were impoverished, or were enriched, and millions of Christian men professing the law of love of their fellows slew one another.

What does all this mean? Why did it happen? What made those people burn houses and slay their fellow men? What were the causes of these events? What force made men act so? These are the instinctive, plain, and most legitimate questions humanity asks itself when it encounters the monuments and tradition of that period.

For a reply to these questions the common sense of mankind turns to the science of history, whose aim is to enable nations and humanity to know themselves.

If history had retained the conception of the ancients it would have said that God, to reward or punish his people, gave Napoleon power and directed his will to the fulfillment of the divine ends, and that reply would have been clear and complete. One might believe or disbelieve in the divine significance of Napoleon, but for anyone believing in it there would have been nothing unintelligible in the history of that period, nor would there have been any contradictions.

But modern history cannot give that reply. Science does not admit the conception of the ancients as to the direct participation of the Deity in human affairs, and therefore history ought to give other answers.

Modern history replying to these questions says: you want to know what this movement means, what caused it, and what force produced these events? Then listen:

"Louis XIV was a very proud and self-confident man; he had such and such mistresses and such and such ministers and he ruled France badly. His descendants were weak men and they too ruled France badly. And they had such and such favorites and such and such mistresses. Moreover, certain men wrote some books at that time. At the end of the eighteenth century there were a couple of dozen men in Paris who began to talk about all men being free and equal. This caused people all over France to begin to slash at and drown one another. They killed the king and many other people. At that time there was in France a man of genius—Napoleon. He conquered everybody everywhere—that is, he killed many people because he was a great genius. And for some reason he went to kill Africans, and killed them so well and was so cunning and wise that when he returned to France he ordered everybody to obey him, and they all obeyed him.

Having become an Emperor he again went out to kill people in Italy, Austria, and Prussia. And there too he killed a great many. In Russia there was an Emperor, Alexander, who decided to restore order in Europe and therefore fought against Napoleon. In 1807 he suddenly made friends with him, but in 1811 they again quarreled and again began killing many people. Napoleon led six hundred thousand men into Russia and captured Moscow; then he suddenly ran away from Moscow, and the Emperor Alexander, helped by the advice of Stein and others, united Europe to arm against the disturber of its peace. All Napoleon's allies suddenly became his enemies and their forces advanced against the fresh forces he raised. The Allies defeated Napoleon, entered Paris, forced Napoleon to abdicate, and sent him to the island of Elba, not depriving him of the title of Emperor and showing him every respect, though five years before and one year later they all regarded him as an outlaw and a brigand. Then Louis XVIII, who till then had been the laughingstock both of the French and the Allies, began to reign. And Napoleon, shedding tears before his Old Guards, renounced the throne and went into exile. Then the skillful statesmen and diplomatists (especially Talleyrand, who managed to sit down in a particular chair before anyone else and thereby extended the frontiers of France) talked in Vienna and by these conversations made the nations happy or unhappy. Suddenly the diplomatists and monarchs nearly quarreled and were on the point of again ordering their armies to kill one another, but just then Napoleon arrived in France with a battalion, and the French, who had been hating him, immediately all submitted to him. But the Allied monarchs were angry at this and went to fight the French once more. And they defeated the genius Napoleon and, suddenly recognizing him as a brigand, sent him to the island of St. Helena. And the exile, separated from the beloved France so dear to his heart, died a lingering death on that rock and bequeathed his great deeds to posterity. But in Europe a reaction occurred and the sovereigns once again all began to oppress their subjects."

It would be a mistake to think that this is ironic—a caricature of the historical accounts. On the contrary it is a very mild expression of the contradictory replies, not meeting the questions, which *all* the historians give, from the compilers of memoirs and the histories of separate states to the writers of general histories and the new histories of the *culture* of that period.

The strangeness and absurdity of these replies arise from the fact that modern history, like a deaf man, answers questions no one has asked.

If the purpose of history be to give a description of the movement of humanity and of the peoples, the first question—in the absence of a reply to which all the rest will be incomprehensible—is: what is the power that moves peoples? To this, modern history laboriously replies either that Napoleon was a great genius, or that Louis XIV was very proud, or that certain writers wrote certain books.

All that may be so and mankind is ready to agree with it, but it is not what was asked. All *that* would be interesting if we recognized a divine power based on itself and always consistently directing its nations through Napoleons, Louis-es, and writers; but we do not acknowledge such a power, and therefore before speaking about Napoleons, Louis-es, and authors, we ought to be shown the connection existing between these men and the movement of the nations.

If instead of a divine power some other force has appeared, it should be explained in what this new force consists, for the whole interest of history lies precisely in that force.

History seems to assume that this force is self-evident and known to everyone. But in spite of every desire to regard it as known, anyone reading many historical works cannot help doubting whether this new force, so variously understood by the historians themselves, is really quite well known to everybody.

CHAPTER II

What force moves the nations?

Biographical historians and historians of separate nations understand this force as a power inherent in heroes and rulers. In their narration events occur solely by the will of a Napoleon, and Alexander, or in general of the persons they describe. The answers given by this kind of historian to the question of what force causes events to happen are satisfactory only as long as there is but one historian to each event. As soon as historians of different nationalities and tendencies begin to describe the same event, the replies they give immediately lose all meaning, for this force is understood by them all not only differently but often in quite contradictory ways. One historian says that an event was produced by Napoleon's power, another that it was produced by Alexander's, a third that it was due to the power of some other person. Besides this, historians of that kind contradict each other even in their statement as to the force on which the authority of some particular person was based. Thiers, a Bonapartist, says that Napoleon's power was based on his virtue and genius. Lanfrey, a Republican, says it was based on his trickery and deception of the people. So the historians of this class, by mutually destroying one another's positions, destroy the understanding of the force which produces events, and furnish no reply to history's essential question.

Writers of universal history who deal with all the nations seem to recognize how erroneous is the specialist historians' view of the force which produces events. They do not recognize it as a power inherent in heroes and rulers, but as the resultant of a multiplicity of variously directed forces. In describing a war or the subjugation of a people, a general historian looks for the cause of the event not in the power of one man, but in the interaction of many persons connected with the event.

According to this view the power of historical personages, represented as the product of many forces, can no longer, it would seem, be regarded as a force that itself produces events. Yet in most cases universal historians still employ the conception of power as a force that itself produces events, and treat it as their cause. In their exposition, an historic character is first the product of his time, and his power only the resultant of various forces, and then his power is itself a force producing events. Gervinus, Schlosser, and others, for instance, at one time prove Napoleon to be a product of the Revolution, of the ideas of 1789 and so forth, and at another plainly say that the campaign of 1812 and other things they do not like were simply the product of Napoleon's misdirected will, and that the very ideas of 1789 were arrested in their development by Napoleon's caprice. The ideas of the Revolution and the general temper of the age produced Napoleon's power. But Napoleon's power suppressed the ideas of the Revolution and the general temper of the age.

This curious contradiction is not accidental. Not only does it occur at every step, but the universal historians' accounts are all made up of a chain of such contradictions. This contradiction occurs because after entering the field of analysis the universal historians stop halfway.

To find component forces equal to the composite or resultant force, the sum of the components must equal the resultant. This condition is never observed by the universal historians, and so to explain the resultant forces they are obliged to admit, in addition to the insufficient components, another unexplained force affecting the resultant action.

Specialist historians describing the campaign of 1813 or the restoration of the Bourbons plainly assert that these events were produced by the will of Alexander. But the universal historian Gervinus, refuting this opinion of the specialist historian, tries to prove that the campaign of 1813 and the restoration of the Bourbons were due to other things beside Alexander's will—such as the activity of Stein, Metternich, Madame de Staël, Talleyrand, Fichte, Chateaubriand, and others. The historian evidently decomposes Alexander's power into the components: Talleyrand, Chateaubriand, and the rest—but the sum of the components, that is, the interactions of Chateaubriand, Talleyrand, Madame de Staël, and the others, evidently does not equal the resultant, namely the phenomenon of millions of Frenchmen submitting to the Bourbons. That Chateaubriand, Madame de Staël, and others spoke certain words to one another only affected their mutual relations but does not account for the submission of millions. And therefore to explain how from these relations of theirs the submission of millions of people resulted—that is, how component forces equal to one A gave a resultant equal to a thousand times A— the historian is again obliged to fall back on power—the force he had denied—and to recognize it as the resultant of the forces, that is, he has to admit an unexplained force acting on the resultant. And that is just what the universal historians do, and consequently they not only contradict the specialist historians but contradict themselves.

Peasants having no clear idea of the cause of rain, say, according to whether they want rain or fine weather: "The wind has blown the clouds away," or, "The wind has brought up the clouds." And in the same way the universal historians sometimes, when it pleases them and fits in with their theory, say that power is the result of events, and sometimes, when they want to prove something else, say that power produces events.

A third class of historians—the so-called historians of culture— following the path laid down by the universal historians who sometimes accept writers and ladies as forces producing events— again take that force to be something quite different. They see it in what is called culture—in mental activity.

The historians of culture are quite consistent in regard to their progenitors, the writers of universal histories, for if historical events may be explained by the fact that certain persons treated one another in such and such ways, why not explain them by the fact that such and such people wrote such and such books? Of the immense number of indications accompanying every vital phenomenon, these historians select the indication of intellectual activity and say that this indication is the cause. But despite their endeavors to prove that the cause of events lies in intellectual activity, only by a great stretch can one admit that there is any connection between intellectual activity and the movement of peoples, and in no case can one admit that intellectual activity controls people's actions, for that view is not confirmed by such facts as the very cruel murders of the French Revolution resulting from the doctrine of the equality of man, or the very cruel wars and executions resulting from the preaching of love.

But even admitting as correct all the cunningly devised arguments with which these histories are filled—admitting that nations are governed by some undefined force called an *idea*—history's essential question still remains unanswered, and to the former power of monarchs and to the influence of advisers and other people introduced by the universal historians, another, newer force—the *idea*—is added, the connection of which with the masses needs explanation. It is possible to understand that Napoleon had power and so events occurred; with some effort one may even conceive that Napoleon together with other influences was the cause of an event; but how a book, *Le Contrat Social*, had the effect of making Frenchmen begin to drown one another cannot be understood without an explanation of the causal nexus of this new force with the event.

Undoubtedly some relation exists between all who live contemporaneously, and so it is possible to find some connection between the intellectual activity of men and their historical movements, just as such a connection may be found between the movements of humanity and commerce, handicraft, gardening, or anything else you please. But why intellectual activity is considered by the historians of culture to be the cause or expression of the whole historical movement is hard to understand. Only the following considerations can have led the historians to such a conclusion: (1) that history is written by learned men, and so it is natural and agreeable for them to think that the activity of their class supplies the basis of the movement of all humanity, just as a similar belief is natural and agreeable to traders, agriculturists, and soldiers (if they do not express it, that is merely because traders and soldiers do not write history), and (2) that spiritual activity, enlightenment, civilization, culture, ideas, are all indistinct, indefinite conceptions under whose banner it is very easy to use words having a still less definite meaning, and which can therefore be readily introduced into any theory.

But not to speak of the intrinsic quality of histories of this kind (which may possibly even be of use to someone for something) the histories of culture, to which all general histories tend more and more to approximate, are significant from the fact that after seriously and minutely examining various religious, philosophic, and political doctrines as causes of events, as soon as they have to describe an actual historic event such as the campaign of 1812 for instance, they involuntarily describe it as resulting from an exercise of power—and say plainly that that was the result of Napoleon's will. Speaking so, the historians of culture involuntarily contradict themselves, and show that the new force they have devised does not account for what happens in history, and that history can only be explained by introducing a power which they apparently do not recognize.

CHAPTER III

A locomotive is moving. Someone asks: "What moves it?" A peasant says the devil moves it. Another man says the locomotive moves because its wheels go round. A third asserts that the cause of its movement lies in the smoke which the wind carries away.

The peasant is irrefutable. He has devised a complete explanation. To refute him someone would have to prove to him that there is no devil, or another peasant would have to explain to him that it is not the devil but a German, who moves the locomotive. Only then, as a result of the contradiction, will they see that they are both wrong. But the man who says that the movement of the wheels is the cause refutes himself, for having once begun to analyze he ought to go on and explain further why the wheels go round; and till he has reached the ultimate cause of the movement of the locomotive in the pressure of steam in the boiler, he has no right to stop in his search for the cause. The man who explains the movement of the locomotive by the smoke that is carried back has noticed that the wheels do not supply an explanation and has taken the first sign that occurs to him and in his turn has offered that as an explanation.

The only conception that can explain the movement of the locomotive is that of a force commensurate with the movement observed.

The only conception that can explain the movement of the peoples is that of some force commensurate with the whole movement of the peoples.

Yet to supply this conception various historians take forces of different kinds, all of which are incommensurate with the movement observed. Some see it as a force directly inherent in heroes, as the peasant sees the devil in the locomotive; others as a force resulting from several other forces, like the movement of the wheels; others again as an intellectual influence, like the smoke that is blown away.

So long as histories are written of separate individuals, whether Caesars, Alexanders, Luthers, or Voltaires, and not the histories of *all*, absolutely *all* those who take part in an event, it is quite impossible to describe the movement of humanity without the conception of a force compelling men to direct their activity toward a certain end. And the only such conception known to historians is that of power.

This conception is the one handle by means of which the material of history, as at present expounded, can be dealt with, and anyone who breaks that handle off, as Buckle did, without finding some other method of treating historical material, merely deprives himself of the one possible way of dealing with it. The necessity of the conception of power as an explanation of historical events is best demonstrated by the universal historians and historians of culture themselves, for they professedly reject that conception but inevitably have recourse to it at every step.

In dealing with humanity's inquiry, the science of history up to now is like money in circulation—paper money and coin. The biographies and special national histories are like paper money. They can be used and can circulate and fulfill their purpose without harm to anyone and even advantageously, as long as no one asks what is the security behind them. You need only forget to ask how the will of heroes produces events, and such histories as Thiers' will be interesting and instructive and may perhaps even possess a tinge of poetry. But just as doubts of the real value of paper money arise either because, being easy to make, too much of it gets made or because people try to exchange it for gold, so also doubts concerning the real value of such histories arise either because too many of them are written or because in his simplicity of heart someone inquires: by what force did Napoleon do this?—that is, wants to exchange the current paper money for the real gold of actual comprehension.

The writers of universal histories and of the history of culture are like people who, recognizing the defects of paper money, decide to substitute for it money made of metal that has not the specific gravity of gold. It may indeed make jingling coin, but will do no more than that. Paper money may deceive the ignorant, but nobody is deceived by tokens of base metal that have no value but merely jingle. As gold is gold only if it is serviceable not merely for exchange but also for use, so universal historians will be valuable only when they can reply to history's essential question: what is power? The universal historians give contradictory replies to that question, while the historians of culture evade it and answer something quite different. And as counters of imitation gold can be used only among a group of people who agree to accept them as gold, or among those who do not know the nature of gold, so universal historians and historians of culture, not answering humanity's essential question, serve as currency for some purposes of their own, only in universities and among the mass of readers who have a taste for what they call "serious reading."

CHAPTER IV

Having abandoned the conception of the ancients as to the divine subjection of the will of a nation to some chosen man and the subjection of that man's will to the Deity, history cannot without contradictions take a single step till it has chosen one of two things: either a return to the former belief in the direct intervention of the Deity in human affairs or a definite explanation of the meaning of the force producing historical events and termed "power."

A return to the first is impossible, the belief has been destroyed; and so it is essential to explain what is meant by power.

Napoleon ordered an army to be raised and go to war. We are so accustomed to that idea and have become so used to it that the question: why did six hundred thousand men go to fight when Napoleon uttered certain words, seems to us senseless. He had the power and so what he ordered was done.

This reply is quite satisfactory if we believe that the power was given him by God. But as soon as we do not admit that, it becomes essential to determine what is this power of one man over others.

It cannot be the direct physical power of a strong man over a weak one—a domination based on the application or threat of physical force, like the power of Hercules; nor can it be based on the effect of moral force, as in their simplicity some historians think who say that the leading figures in history are heroes, that is, men gifted with a special strength of soul and mind called genius. This power cannot be based on the predominance of moral strength, for, not to mention heroes such as Napoleon about whose moral qualities opinions differ widely, history shows us that neither a Louis XI nor a Metternich, who ruled over millions of people, had any particular moral qualities, but on the contrary were generally morally weaker than any of the millions they ruled over.

If the source of power lies neither in the physical nor in the moral qualities of him who possesses it, it must evidently be looked for elsewhere—in the relation to the people of the man who wields the power.

And that is how power is understood by the science of jurisprudence, that exchange bank of history which offers to exchange history's understanding of power for true gold.

Power is the collective will of the people transferred, by expressed or tacit consent, to their chosen rulers.

In the domain of jurisprudence, which consists of discussions of how a state and power might be arranged were it possible for all that to be arranged, it is all very clear; but when applied to history that definition of power needs explanation.

The science of jurisprudence regards the state and power as the ancients regarded fire—namely, as something existing absolutely. But for history, the state and power are merely phenomena, just as for modern physics fire is not an element but a phenomenon.

From this fundamental difference between the view held by history and that held by jurisprudence, it follows that jurisprudence can tell minutely how in its opinion power should be constituted and what power—existing immutably outside time—is, but to history's questions about the meaning of the mutations of power *in* time it can answer nothing.

If power be the collective will of the people transferred to their ruler, was Pugachëv a representative of the will of the people? If not, then why was Napoleon I? Why was Napoleon III a criminal when he was taken prisoner at Boulogne, and why, later on, were those criminals whom he arrested?

Do palace revolutions—in which sometimes only two or three people take part—transfer the will of the people to a new ruler? In international relations, is the will of the people also transferred to their conqueror? Was the will of the Confederation of the Rhine transferred to Napoleon in 1806? Was the will of the Russian people transferred to Napoleon in 1809, when our army in alliance with the French went to fight the Austrians?

To these questions three answers are possible:

Either to assume (1) that the will of the people is always unconditionally transferred to the ruler or rulers they have chosen, and that therefore every emergence of a new power, every struggle against the power once appointed, should be absolutely regarded as an infringement of the real power; or (2) that the will of the people is transferred to the rulers conditionally, under definite and known conditions, and to show that all limitations, conflicts, and even destructions of power result from a nonobservance by the rulers of the conditions under which their power was entrusted to them; or (3) that the will of the people is delegated to the rulers conditionally, but that the conditions are unknown and indefinite, and that the appearance of several authorities, their struggles and their falls, result solely from the greater or lesser fulfillment by the rulers of these unknown conditions on which the will of the people is transferred from some people to others.

And these are the three ways in which the historians do explain the relation of the people to their rulers.

Some historians—those biographical and specialist historians already referred to—in their simplicity failing to understand the question of the meaning of power, seem to consider that the collective will of the people is unconditionally transferred to historical persons, and therefore when describing some single state they assume that particular power to be the one absolute and real power, and that any other force opposing this is not a power but a violation of power—mere violence.

Their theory, suitable for primitive and peaceful periods of history, has the inconvenience—in application to complex and stormy periods in the life of nations during which various powers arise simultaneously and struggle with one another—that a Legitimist historian will prove that the National Convention, the Directory, and Bonaparte were mere infringers of the true power, while a Republican and a Bonapartist will prove: the one that the Convention and the other that the Empire was the real power, and that all the others were violations of power. Evidently the explanations furnished by these historians being mutually contradictory can only satisfy young children.

Recognizing the falsity of this view of history, another set of historians say that power rests on a conditional delegation of the will of the people to their rulers, and that historical leaders have power only conditionally on carrying out the program that the will of the people has by tacit agreement prescribed to them. But what this program consists in these historians do not say, or if they do they continually contradict one another.

Each historian, according to his view of what constitutes a nation's progress, looks for these conditions in the greatness, wealth, freedom, or enlightenment of citizens of France or some other country. But not to mention the historians' contradictions as to the nature of this program—or even admitting that some one general program of these conditions exists—the facts of history almost always contradict that theory. If the conditions under which power is entrusted consist in the wealth, freedom, and enlightenment of the people, how is it that Louis XIV and Iván the Terrible end their reigns tranquilly, while Louis XVI and Charles I are executed by their people? To this question historians reply that Louis XIV's activity, contrary to the program, reacted on Louis XVI. But why did it not react on Louis XIV or on Louis XV—why should it react just on Louis XVI? And what is the time limit for such reactions? To these questions there are and can be no answers. Equally little does this view explain why for several centuries the collective will is not withdrawn from certain rulers and their heirs, and then suddenly during a period of fifty years is transferred to the Convention, to the Directory, to Napoleon, to Alexander, to Louis XVIII, to Napoleon again, to Charles X, to Louis Philippe, to a Republican government, and to Napoleon III. When explaining these rapid transfers of the people's will from one individual to another, especially in view of international relations, conquests, and alliances, the historians are obliged to admit that some of these transfers are not normal delegations of the people's will but are accidents dependent on cunning, on mistakes, on craft, or on the weakness of a diplomatist, a ruler, or a party leader. So that the greater part of the events of history—civil wars, revolutions, and conquests—are presented by these historians not as the results of free transferences of the people's will, but as results of the ill-directed will of one or more individuals, that is, once again, as usurpations of power. And so these historians also see and admit historical events which are exceptions to the theory.

These historians resemble a botanist who, having noticed that some plants grow from seeds producing two cotyledons, should insist that all that grows does so by sprouting into two leaves, and that the palm, the mushroom, and even the oak, which blossom into full growth and no longer resemble two leaves, are deviations from the theory.

Historians of the third class assume that the will of the people is transferred to historic personages conditionally, but that the conditions are unknown to us. They say that historical personages have power only because they fulfill the will of the people which has been delegated to them.

But in that case, if the force that moves nations lies not in the historic leaders but in the nations themselves, what significance have those leaders?

The leaders, these historians tell us, express the will of the people: the activity of the leaders represents the activity of the people.

But in that case the question arises whether all the activity of the leaders serves as an expression of the people's will or only some part of it. If the whole activity of the leaders serves as the expression of the people's will, as some historians suppose, then all the details of the court scandals contained in the biographies of a Napoleon or a Catherine serve to express the life of the nation, which is evident nonsense; but if it is only some particular side of the activity of an historical leader which serves to express the people's life, as other so-called "philosophical" historians believe, then to determine which side of the activity of a leader expresses the nation's life, we have first of all to know in what the nation's life consists.

Met by this difficulty historians of that class devise some most obscure, impalpable, and general abstraction which can cover all conceivable occurrences, and declare this abstraction to be the aim of humanity's movement. The most usual generalizations adopted by almost all the historians are: freedom, equality, enlightenment, progress, civilization, and culture. Postulating some generalization as the goal of the movement of humanity, the historians study the men of whom the greatest number of monuments have remained: kings, ministers, generals, authors, reformers, popes, and journalists, to the extent to which in their opinion these persons have promoted or hindered that abstraction. But as it is in no way proved that the aim of humanity does consist in freedom, equality, enlightenment, or civilization, and as the connection of the people with the rulers and enlighteners of humanity is only based on the arbitrary assumption that the collective will of the people is always transferred to the men whom we have noticed, it happens that the activity of the millions who migrate, burn houses, abandon agriculture, and destroy one another never is expressed in the account of the activity of some dozen people who did not burn houses, practice agriculture, or slay their fellow creatures.

History proves this at every turn. Is the ferment of the peoples of the west at the end of the eighteenth century and their drive eastward explained by the activity of Louis XIV, XV, and XVI, their mistresses and ministers, and by the lives of Napoleon, Rousseau, Diderot, Beaumarchais, and others?

Is the movement of the Russian people eastward to Kazán and Siberia expressed by details of the morbid character of Iván the Terrible and by his correspondence with Kúrbski?

Is the movement of the peoples at the time of the Crusades explained by the life and activity of the Godfreys and the Louis-es and their ladies? For us that movement of the peoples from west to east, without leaders, with a crowd of vagrants, and with Peter the Hermit, remains incomprehensible. And yet more incomprehensible is the cessation of that movement when a rational and sacred aim for the Crusade—the deliverance of Jerusalem—had been clearly defined by historic leaders. Popes, kings, and knights incited the peoples to free the Holy Land; but the people did not go, for the unknown cause which had previously impelled them to go no longer existed. The history of the Godfreys and the Minnesingers can evidently not cover the life of the peoples. And the history of the Godfreys and the Minnesingers has remained the history of Godfreys and Minnesingers, but the history of the life of the peoples and their impulses has remained unknown.

Still less does the history of authors and reformers explain to us the life of the peoples.

The history of culture explains to us the impulses and conditions of life and thought of a writer or a reformer. We learn that Luther had a hot temper and said such and such things; we learn that Rousseau was suspicious and wrote such and such books; but we do not learn why after the Reformation the peoples massacred one another, nor why during the French Revolution they guillotined one another.

If we unite both these kinds of history, as is done by the newest historians, we shall have the history of monarchs and writers, but not the history of the life of the peoples.

CHAPTER V

The life of the nations is not contained in the lives of a few men, for the connection between those men and the nations has not been found. The theory that this connection is based on the transference of the collective will of a people to certain historical personages is an hypothesis unconfirmed by the experience of history.

The theory of the transference of the collective will of the people to historic persons may perhaps explain much in the domain of jurisprudence and be essential for its purposes, but in its application to history, as soon as revolutions, conquests, or civil wars occur— that is, as soon as history begins—that theory explains nothing.

The theory seems irrefutable just because the act of transference of the people's will cannot be verified, for it never occurred.

Whatever happens and whoever may stand at the head of affairs, the theory can always say that such and such a person took the lead because the collective will was transferred to him.

The replies this theory gives to historical questions are like the replies of a man who, watching the movements of a herd of cattle and paying no attention to the varying quality of the pasturage in different parts of the field, or to the driving of the herdsman, should attribute the direction the herd takes to what animal happens to be at its head.

"The herd goes in that direction because the animal in front leads it and the collective will of all the other animals is vested in that leader." This is what historians of the first class say—those who assume the unconditional transference of the people's will.

"If the animals leading the herd change, this happens because the collective will of all the animals is transferred from one leader to another, according to whether the animal is or is not leading them in the direction selected by the whole herd." Such is the reply historians who assume that the collective will of the people is delegated to rulers under conditions which they regard as known. (With this method of observation it often happens that the observer, influenced by the direction he himself prefers, regards those as leaders who, owing to the people's change of direction, are no longer in front, but on one side, or even in the rear.)

"If the animals in front are continually changing and the direction of the whole herd is constantly altered, this is because in order to follow a given direction the animals transfer their will to the animals that have attracted our attention, and to study the movements of the herd we must watch the movements of all the prominent animals moving on all sides of the herd." So say the third class of historians who regard all historical persons, from monarchs to journalists, as the expression of their age.

The theory of the transference of the will of the people to historic persons is merely a paraphrase—a restatement of the question in other words.

What causes historical events? Power. What is power? Power is the collective will of the people transferred to one person. Under what condition is the will of the people delegated to one person? On condition that that person expresses the will of the whole people. That is, power is power: in other words, power is a word the meaning of which we do not understand.

If the realm of human knowledge were confined to abstract reasoning, then having subjected to criticism the explanation of "power" that juridical science gives us, humanity would conclude that power is merely a word and has no real existence. But to understand phenomena man has, besides abstract reasoning, experience by which he verifies his reflections. And experience tells us that power is not merely a word but an actually existing phenomenon.

Not to speak of the fact that no description of the collective activity of men can do without the conception of power, the existence of power is proved both by history and by observing contemporary events.

Whenever an event occurs a man appears or men appear, by whose will the event seems to have taken place. Napoleon III issues a decree and the French go to Mexico. The King of Prussia and Bismarck issue decrees and an army enters Bohemia. Napoleon I issues a decree and an army enters Russia. Alexander I gives a command and the French submit to the Bourbons. Experience shows us that whatever event occurs it is always related to the will of one or of several men who have decreed it.

The historians, in accord with the old habit of acknowledging divine intervention in human affairs, want to see the cause of events in the expression of the will of someone endowed with power, but that supposition is not confirmed either by reason or by experience.

On the one side reflection shows that the expression of a man's will—his words—are only part of the general activity expressed in an event, as for instance in a war or a revolution, and so without assuming an incomprehensible, supernatural force—a miracle—one cannot admit that words can be the immediate cause of the movements of millions of men. On the other hand, even if we admitted that words could be the cause of events, history shows that the expression of the will of historical personages does not in most cases produce any effect, that is to say, their commands are often not executed, and sometimes the very opposite of what they order occurs.

Without admitting divine intervention in the affairs of humanity we cannot regard "power" as the cause of events.

Power, from the standpoint of experience, is merely the relation that exists between the expression of someone's will and the execution of that will by others.

To explain the conditions of that relationship we must first establish a conception of the expression of will, referring it to man and not to the Deity.

If the Deity issues a command, expresses His will, as ancient history tells us, the expression of that will is independent of time and is not caused by anything, for the Divinity is not controlled by an event. But speaking of commands that are the expression of the will of men acting in time and in relation to one another, to explain the connection of commands with events we must restore: (1) the condition of all that takes place: the continuity of movement in time both of the events and of the person who commands, and (2) the inevitability of the connection between the person commanding and those who execute his command.

CHAPTER VI

O nly the expression of the will of the Deity, not dependent on time, can relate to a whole series of events occurring over a period of years or centuries, and only the Deity, independent of everything, can by His sole will determine the direction of humanity's movement; but man acts in time and himself takes part in what occurs.

Reinstating the first condition omitted, that of time, we see that no command can be executed without some preceding order having been given rendering the execution of the last command possible.

No command ever appears spontaneously, or itself covers a whole series of occurrences; but each command follows from another, and never refers to a whole series of events but always to one moment only of an event.

When, for instance, we say that Napoleon ordered armies to go to war, we combine in one simultaneous expression a whole series of consecutive commands dependent one on another. Napoleon could not have commanded an invasion of Russia and never did so. Today he ordered such and such papers to be written to Vienna, to Berlin, and to Petersburg; tomorrow such and such decrees and orders to the army, the fleet, the commissariat, and so on and so on—millions of commands, which formed a whole series corresponding to a series of events which brought the French armies into Russia.

If throughout his reign Napoleon gave commands concerning an invasion of England and expended on no other undertaking so much time and effort, and yet during his whole reign never once attempted to execute that design but undertook an expedition into Russia, with which country he considered it desirable to be in alliance (a conviction he repeatedly expressed)—this came about because his commands did not correspond to the course of events in the first case, but did so correspond in the latter.

For an order to be certainly executed, it is necessary that a man should order what can be executed. But to know what can and what cannot be executed is impossible, not only in the case of Napoleon's invasion of Russia in which millions participated, but even in the simplest event, for in either case millions of obstacles may arise to prevent its execution. Every order executed is always one of an immense number unexecuted. All the impossible orders inconsistent with the course of events remain unexecuted. Only the possible ones get linked up with a consecutive series of commands corresponding to a series of events, and are executed.

Our false conception that an event is caused by a command which precedes it is due to the fact that when the event has taken place and out of thousands of others those few commands which were consistent with that event have been executed, we forget about the others that were not executed because they could not be. Apart from that, the chief source of our error in this matter is due to the fact that in the historical accounts a whole series of innumerable, diverse, and petty events, such for instance as all those which led the French armies to Russia, is generalized into one event in accord with the result produced by that series of events, and corresponding with this generalization the whole series of commands is also generalized into a single expression of will.

We say that Napoleon wished to invade Russia and invaded it. In reality in all Napoleon's activity we never find anything resembling an expression of that wish, but find a series of orders, or expressions of his will, very variously and indefinitely directed. Amid a long series of unexecuted orders of Napoleon's one series, for the campaign of 1812, was carried out—not because those orders differed in any way from the other, unexecuted orders but because they coincided with the course of events that led the French army into Russia; just as in stencil work this or that figure comes out not because the color was laid on from this side or in that way, but because it was laid on from all sides over the figure cut in the stencil.

So that examining the relation in time of the commands to the events, we find that a command can never be the cause of the event, but that a certain definite dependence exists between the two.

To understand in what this dependence consists it is necessary to reinstate another omitted condition of every command proceeding not from the Deity but from a man, which is, that the man who gives the command himself takes part in the event.

This relation of the commander to those he commands is just what is called power. This relation consists in the following:

For common action people always unite in certain combinations, in which regardless of the difference of the aims set for the common action, the relation between those taking part in it is always the same.

Men uniting in these combinations always assume such relations toward one another that the larger number take a more direct share, and the smaller number a less direct share, in the collective action for which they have combined.

Of all the combinations in which men unite for collective action one of the most striking and definite examples is an army.

Every army is composed of lower grades of the service—the rank and file—of whom there are always the greatest number; of the next higher military rank—corporals and noncommissioned officers of whom there are fewer, and of still-higher officers of whom there are still fewer, and so on to the highest military command which is concentrated in one person.

A military organization may be quite correctly compared to a cone, of which the base with the largest diameter consists of the rank and file; the next higher and smaller section of the cone consists of the next higher grades of the army, and so on to the apex, the point of which will represent the commander in chief.

The soldiers, of whom there are the most, form the lower section of the cone and its base. The soldier himself does the stabbing, hacking, burning, and pillaging, and always receives orders for these actions from men above him; he himself never gives an order. The noncommissioned officers (of whom there are fewer) perform the action itself less frequently than the soldiers, but they already give commands. An officer still less often acts directly himself, but commands still more frequently. A general does nothing but command the troops, indicates the objective, and hardly ever uses a weapon himself. The commander in chief never takes direct part in the action itself, but only gives general orders concerning the movement of the mass of the troops. A similar relation of people to one another is seen in every combination of men for common activity—in agriculture, trade, and every administration.

And so without particularly analyzing all the contiguous sections of a cone and of the ranks of an army, or the ranks and positions in any administrative or public business whatever from the lowest to the highest, we see a law by which men, to take associated action, combine in such relations that the more directly they participate in performing the action the less they can command and the more numerous they are, while the less their direct participation in the action itself, the more they command and the fewer of them there are; rising in this way from the lowest ranks to the man at the top, who takes the least direct share in the action and directs his activity chiefly to commanding.

This relation of the men who command to those they command is what constitutes the essence of the conception called power.

Having restored the condition of time under which all events occur, we find that a command is executed only when it is related to a corresponding series of events. Restoring the essential condition of relation between those who command and those who execute, we find that by the very nature of the case those who command take the smallest part in the action itself and that their activity is exclusively directed to commanding.

CHAPTER VII

When an event is taking place people express their opinions and wishes about it, and as the event results from the collective activity of many people, some one of the opinions or wishes expressed is sure to be fulfilled if but approximately. When one of the opinions expressed is fulfilled, that opinion gets connected with the event as a command preceding it.

Men are hauling a log. Each of them expresses his opinion as to how and where to haul it. They haul the log away, and it happens that this is done as one of them said. He *ordered* it. There we have command and power in their primary form. The man who worked most with his hands could not think so much about what he was doing, or reflect on or command what would result from the common activity; while the man who commanded more would evidently work less with his hands on account of his greater verbal activity.

When some larger concourse of men direct their activity to a common aim there is a yet sharper division of those who, because their activity is given to directing and commanding, take less part in the direct work.

When a man works alone he always has a certain set of reflections which as it seems to him directed his past activity, justify his present activity, and guide him in planning his future actions. Just the same is done by a concourse of people, allowing those who do not take a direct part in the activity to devise considerations, justifications, and surmises concerning their collective activity.

For reasons known or unknown to us the French began to drown and kill one another. And corresponding to the event its justification appears in people's belief that this was necessary for the welfare of France, for liberty, and for equality. People ceased to kill one another, and this event was accompanied by its justification in the necessity for a centralization of power, resistance to Europe, and so on. Men went from the west to the east killing their fellow men, and the event was accompanied by phrases about the glory of France, the baseness of England, and so on. History shows us that these justifications of the events have no common sense and are all contradictory, as in the case of killing a man as the result of recognizing his rights, and the killing of millions in Russia for the humiliation of England. But these justifications have a very necessary significance in their own day.

These justifications release those who produce the events from moral responsibility. These temporary aims are like the broom fixed in front of a locomotive to clear the snow from the rails in front: they clear men's moral responsibilities from their path.

Without such justification there would be no reply to the simplest question that presents itself when examining each historical event. How is it that millions of men commit collective crimes—make war, commit murder, and so on?

With the present complex forms of political and social life in Europe can any event that is not prescribed, decreed, or ordered by monarchs, ministers, parliaments, or newspapers be imagined? Is there any collective action which cannot find its justification in political unity, in patriotism, in the balance of power, or in civilization? So that every event that occurs inevitably coincides with some expressed wish and, receiving a justification, presents itself as the result of the will of one man or of several men.

In whatever direction a ship moves, the flow of the waves it cuts will always be noticeable ahead of it. To those on board the ship the movement of those waves will be the only perceptible motion.

Only by watching closely moment by moment the movement of that flow and comparing it with the movement of the ship do we convince ourselves that every bit of it is occasioned by the forward movement of the ship, and that we were led into error by the fact that we ourselves were imperceptibly moving.

We see the same if we watch moment by moment the movement of historical characters (that is, re-establish the inevitable condition of all that occurs—the continuity of movement in time) and do not lose sight of the essential connection of historical persons with the masses.

When the ship moves in one direction there is one and the same wave ahead of it, when it turns frequently the wave ahead of it also turns frequently. But wherever it may turn there always will be the wave anticipating its movement.

Whatever happens it always appears that just that event was foreseen and decreed. Wherever the ship may go, the rush of water which neither directs nor increases its movement foams ahead of it, and at a distance seems to us not merely to move of itself but to govern the ship's movement also.

Examining only those expressions of the will of historical persons which, as commands, were related to events, historians have assumed that the events depended on those commands. But examining the events themselves and the connection in which the historical persons stood to the people, we have found that they and their orders were dependent on events. The incontestable proof of this deduction is that, however many commands were issued, the event does not take place unless there are other causes for it, but as soon as an event occurs—be it what it may—then out of all the continually expressed wishes of different people some will always be found which by their meaning and their time of utterance are related as commands to the events.

Arriving at this conclusion we can reply directly and positively to these two essential questions of history:

(1) What is power?

(2) What force produces the movement of the nations?

(1) Power is the relation of a given person to other individuals, in which the more this person expresses opinions, predictions, and justifications of the collective action that is performed, the less is his participation in that action.

(2) The movement of nations is caused not by power, nor by intellectual activity, nor even by a combination of the two as historians have supposed, but by the activity of *all* the people who participate in the events, and who always combine in such a way that those taking the largest direct share in the event take on themselves the least responsibility and vice versa.

Morally the wielder of power appears to cause the event; physically it is those who submit to the power. But as the moral activity is inconceivable without the physical, the cause of the event is neither in the one nor in the other but in the union of the two.

Or in other words, the conception of a cause is inapplicable to the phenomena we are examining.

In the last analysis we reach the circle of infinity—that final limit to which in every domain of thought man's reason arrives if it is not playing with the subject. Electricity produces heat, heat produces electricity. Atoms attract each other and atoms repel one another.

Speaking of the interaction of heat and electricity and of atoms, we cannot say why this occurs, and we say that it is so because it is inconceivable otherwise, because it must be so and that it is a law. The same applies to historical events. Why war and revolution occur we do not know. We only know that to produce the one or the other action, people combine in a certain formation in which they all take part, and we say that this is so because it is unthinkable otherwise, or in other words that it is a law.

CHAPTER VIII

If history dealt only with external phenomena, the establishment of this simple and obvious law would suffice and we should have finished our argument. But the law of history relates to man. A particle of matter cannot tell us that it does not feel the law of attraction or repulsion and that that law is untrue, but man, who is the subject of history, says plainly: I am free and am therefore not subject to the law.

The presence of the problem of man's free will, though unexpressed, is felt at every step of history.

All seriously thinking historians have involuntarily encountered this question. All the contradictions and obscurities of history and the false path historical science has followed are due solely to the lack of a solution of that question.

If the will of every man were free, that is, if each man could act as he pleased, all history would be a series of disconnected incidents.

If in a thousand years even one man in a million could act freely, that is, as he chose, it is evident that one single free act of that man's in violation of the laws governing human action would destroy the possibility of the existence of any laws for the whole of humanity.

If there be a single law governing the actions of men, free will cannot exist, for then man's will is subject to that law.

In this contradiction lies the problem of free will, which from most ancient times has occupied the best human minds and from most ancient times has been presented in its whole tremendous significance.

The problem is that regarding man as a subject of observation from whatever point of view—theological, historical, ethical, or philosophic—we find a general law of necessity to which he (like all that exists) is subject. But regarding him from within ourselves as what we are conscious of, we feel ourselves to be free.

This consciousness is a source of self-cognition quite apart from and independent of reason. Through his reason man observes himself, but only through consciousness does he know himself.

Apart from consciousness of self no observation or application of reason is conceivable.

To understand, observe, and draw conclusions, man must first of all be conscious of himself as living. A man is only conscious of himself as a living being by the fact that he wills, that is, is conscious of his volition. But his will—which forms the essence of his life—man recognizes (and can but recognize) as free.

If, observing himself, man sees that his will is always directed by one and the same law (whether he observes the necessity of taking food, using his brain, or anything else) he cannot recognize this never-varying direction of his will otherwise than as a limitation of it. Were it not free it could not be limited. A man's will seems to him to be limited just because he is not conscious of it except as free.

You say: I am not free. But I have lifted my hand and let it fall. Everyone understands that this illogical reply is an irrefutable demonstration of freedom.

That reply is the expression of a consciousness that is not subject to reason.

If the consciousness of freedom were not a separate and independent source of self-consciousness it would be subject to reasoning and to experience, but in fact such subjection does not exist and is inconceivable.

A series of experiments and arguments proves to every man that he, as an object of observation, is subject to certain laws, and man submits to them and never resists the laws of gravity or impermeability once he has become acquainted with them. But the same series of experiments and arguments proves to him that the complete freedom of which he is conscious in himself is impossible, and that his every action depends on his organization, his character, and the motives acting upon him; yet man never submits to the deductions of these experiments and arguments. Having learned from experiment and argument that a stone falls downwards, a man indubitably believes this and always expects the law that he has learned to be fulfilled.

But learning just as certainly that his will is subject to laws, he does not and cannot believe this.

However often experiment and reasoning may show a man that under the same conditions and with the same character he will do the same thing as before, yet when under the same conditions and with the same character he approaches for the thousandth time the action that always ends in the same way, he feels as certainly convinced as before the experiment that he can act as he pleases. Every man, savage or sage, however incontestably reason and experiment may prove to him that it is impossible to imagine two different courses of action in precisely the same conditions, feels that without this irrational conception (which constitutes the essence of freedom) he cannot imagine life. He feels that however impossible it may be, it is so, for without this conception of freedom not only would he be unable to understand life, but he would be unable to live for a single moment.

He could not live, because all man's efforts, all his impulses to life, are only efforts to increase freedom. Wealth and poverty, fame and obscurity, power and subordination, strength and weakness, health and disease, culture and ignorance, work and leisure, repletion and hunger, virtue and vice, are only greater or lesser degrees of freedom.

A man having no freedom cannot be conceived of except as deprived of life.

If the conception of freedom appears to reason to be a senseless contradiction like the possibility of performing two actions at one and the same instant of time, or of an effect without a cause, that only proves that consciousness is not subject to reason.

This unshakable, irrefutable consciousness of freedom, uncontrolled by experiment or argument, recognized by all thinkers and felt by everyone without exception, this consciousness without which no conception of man is possible constitutes the other side of the question.

Man is the creation of an all-powerful, all-good, and all-seeing God. What is sin, the conception of which arises from the consciousness of man's freedom? That is a question for theology.

The actions of men are subject to general immutable laws expressed in statistics. What is man's responsibility to society, the conception of which results from the conception of freedom? That is a question for jurisprudence.

Man's actions proceed from his innate character and the motives acting upon him. What is conscience and the perception of right and wrong in actions that follows from the consciousness of freedom? That is a question for ethics.

Man in connection with the general life of humanity appears subject to laws which determine that life. But the same man apart from that connection appears to be free. How should the past life of nations and of humanity be regarded—as the result of the free, or as the result of the constrained, activity of man? That is a question for history.

Only in our self-confident day of the popularization of knowledge—thanks to that most powerful engine of ignorance, the diffusion of printed matter—has the question of the freedom of will been put on a level on which the question itself cannot exist. In our time the majority of so-called advanced people—that is, the crowd of ignoramuses—have taken the work of the naturalists who deal with one side of the question for a solution of the whole problem.

They say and write and print that the soul and freedom do not exist, for the life of man is expressed by muscular movements and muscular movements are conditioned by the activity of the nerves; the soul and free will do not exist because at an unknown period of time we sprang from the apes. They say this, not at all suspecting that thousands of years ago that same law of necessity which with such ardor they are now trying to prove by physiology and comparative zoology was not merely acknowledged by all the religions and all the thinkers, but has never been denied. They do not see that the role of the natural sciences in this matter is merely to serve as an instrument for the illumination of one side of it. For the fact that, from the point of view of observation, reason and the will are merely secretions of the brain, and that man following the general law may have developed from lower animals at some unknown period of time, only explains from a fresh side the truth admitted thousands of years ago by all the religious and philosophic theories—that from the point of view of reason man is subject to the law of necessity; but it does not advance by a hair's breadth the solution of the question, which has another, opposite, side, based on the consciousness of freedom.

If men descended from the apes at an unknown period of time, that is as comprehensible as that they were made from a handful of earth at a certain period of time (in the first case the unknown quantity is the time, in the second case it is the origin); and the question of how man's consciousness of freedom is to be reconciled with the law of necessity to which he is subject cannot be solved by comparative physiology and zoology, for in a frog, a rabbit, or an ape, we can observe only the muscular nervous activity, but in man we observe consciousness as well as the muscular and nervous activity.

The naturalists and their followers, thinking they can solve this question, are like plasterers set to plaster one side of the walls of a church who, availing themselves of the absence of the chief superintendent of the work, should in an access of zeal plaster over the windows, icons, woodwork, and still unbuttressed walls, and should be delighted that from their point of view as plasterers, everything is now so smooth and regular.

CHAPTER IX

For the solution of the question of free will or inevitability, history has this advantage over other branches of knowledge in which the question is dealt with, that for history this question does not refer to the essence of man's free will but its manifestation in the past and under certain conditions.

In regard to this question, history stands to the other sciences as experimental science stands to abstract science.

The subject for history is not man's will itself but our presentation of it.

And so for history, the insoluble mystery presented by the incompatibility of free will and inevitability does not exist as it does for theology, ethics, and philosophy. History surveys a presentation of man's life in which the union of these two contradictions has already taken place.

In actual life each historic event, each human action, is very clearly and definitely understood without any sense of contradiction, although each event presents itself as partly free and partly compulsory.

To solve the question of how freedom and necessity are combined and what constitutes the essence of these two conceptions, the philosophy of history can and should follow a path contrary to that taken by other sciences. Instead of first defining the conceptions of freedom and inevitability in themselves, and then ranging the phenomena of life under those definitions, history should deduce a definition of the conception of freedom and inevitability themselves from the immense quantity of phenomena of which it is cognizant and that always appear dependent on these two elements.

Whatever presentation of the activity of many men or of an individual we may consider, we always regard it as the result partly of man's free will and partly of the law of inevitability.

Whether we speak of the migration of the peoples and the incursions of the barbarians, or of the decrees of Napoleon III, or of someone's action an hour ago in choosing one direction out of several for his walk, we are unconscious of any contradiction. The degree of freedom and inevitability governing the actions of these people is clearly defined for us.

Our conception of the degree of freedom often varies according to differences in the point of view from which we regard the event, but every human action appears to us as a certain combination of freedom and inevitability. In every action we examine we see a certain measure of freedom and a certain measure of inevitability. And always the more freedom we see in any action the less inevitability do we perceive, and the more inevitability the less freedom.

The proportion of freedom to inevitability decreases and increases according to the point of view from which the action is regarded, but their relation is always one of inverse proportion.

A sinking man who clutches at another and drowns him; or a hungry mother exhausted by feeding her baby, who steals some food; or a man trained to discipline who on duty at the word of command kills a defenseless man—seem less guilty, that is, less free and more subject to the law of necessity, to one who knows the circumstances in which these people were placed, and more free to one who does not know that the man was himself drowning, that the mother was hungry, that the soldier was in the ranks, and so on. Similarly a man who committed a murder twenty years ago and has since lived peaceably and harmlessly in society seems less guilty and his action more due to the law of inevitability, to someone who considers his action after twenty years have elapsed than to one who examined it the day after it was committed. And in the same way every action of an insane, intoxicated, or highly excited man appears less free and more inevitable to one who knows the mental condition of him who committed the action, and seems more free and less inevitable to one who does not know it. In all these cases the conception of freedom is increased or diminished and the conception of compulsion is correspondingly decreased or increased, according to the point of view from which the action is regarded. So that the greater the conception of necessity the smaller the conception of freedom and vice versa.

Religion, the common sense of mankind, the science of jurisprudence, and history itself understand alike this relation between necessity and freedom.

All cases without exception in which our conception of freedom and necessity is increased and diminished depend on three considerations:

(1) The relation to the external world of the man who commits the deeds.

(2) His relation to time.

(3) His relation to the causes leading to the action.

The first consideration is the clearness of our perception of the man's relation to the external world and the greater or lesser clearness of our understanding of the definite position occupied by the man in relation to everything coexisting with him. This is what makes it evident that a drowning man is less free and more subject to necessity than one standing on dry ground, and that makes the actions of a man closely connected with others in a thickly populated district, or of one bound by family, official, or business duties, seem certainly less free and more subject to necessity than those of a man living in solitude and seclusion.

If we consider a man alone, apart from his relation to everything around him, each action of his seems to us free. But if we see his relation to anything around him, if we see his connection with anything whatever—with a man who speaks to him, a book he reads, the work on which he is engaged, even with the air he breathes or the light that falls on the things about him—we see that each of these circumstances has an influence on him and controls at least some side of his activity. And the more we perceive of these influences the more our conception of his freedom diminishes and the more our conception of the necessity that weighs on him increases.

The second consideration is the more or less evident time relation of the man to the world and the clearness of our perception of the place the man's action occupies in time. That is the ground which makes the fall of the first man, resulting in the production of the human race, appear evidently less free than a man's entry into marriage today. It is the reason why the life and activity of people who lived centuries ago and are connected with me in time cannot seem to me as free as the life of a contemporary, the consequences of which are still unknown to me.

The degree of our conception of freedom or inevitability depends in this respect on the greater or lesser lapse of time between the performance of the action and our judgment of it.

If I examine an act I performed a moment ago in approximately the same circumstances as those I am in now, my action appears to me undoubtedly free. But if I examine an act performed a month ago, then being in different circumstances, I cannot help recognizing that if that act had not been committed much that resulted from it—good, agreeable, and even essential—would not have taken place. If I reflect on an action still more remote, ten years ago or more, then the consequences of my action are still plainer to me and I find it hard to imagine what would have happened had that action not been performed. The farther I go back in memory, or what is the same thing the farther I go forward in my judgment, the more doubtful becomes my belief in the freedom of my action.

In history we find a very similar progress of conviction concerning the part played by free will in the general affairs of humanity. A contemporary event seems to us to be indubitably the doing of all the known participants, but with a more remote event we already see its inevitable results which prevent our considering anything else possible. And the farther we go back in examining events the less arbitrary do they appear.

The Austro-Prussian war appears to us undoubtedly the result of the crafty conduct of Bismarck, and so on. The Napoleonic wars still seem to us, though already questionably, to be the outcome of their heroes' will. But in the Crusades we already see an event occupying its definite place in history and without which we cannot imagine the modern history of Europe, though to the chroniclers of the Crusades that event appeared as merely due to the will of certain people. In regard to the migration of the peoples it does not enter anyone's head today to suppose that the renovation of the European world depended on Attila's caprice. The farther back in history the object of our observation lies, the more doubtful does the free will of those concerned in the event become and the more manifest the law of inevitability.

The third consideration is the degree to which we apprehend that endless chain of causation inevitably demanded by reason, in which each phenomenon comprehended, and therefore man's every action, must have its definite place as a result of what has gone before and as a cause of what will follow.

The better we are acquainted with the physiological, psychological, and historical laws deduced by observation and by which man is controlled, and the more correctly we perceive the physiological, psychological, and historical causes of the action, and the simpler the action we are observing and the less complex the character and mind of the man in question, the more subject to inevitability and the less free do our actions and those of others appear.

When we do not at all understand the cause of an action, whether a crime, a good action, or even one that is simply nonmoral, we ascribe a greater amount of freedom to it. In the case of a crime we most urgently demand the punishment for such an act; in the case of a virtuous act we rate its merit most highly. In an indifferent case we recognize in it more individuality, originality, and independence. But if even one of the innumerable causes of the act is known to us we recognize a certain element of necessity and are less insistent on punishment for the crime, or the acknowledgment of the merit of the virtuous act, or the freedom of the apparently original action. That a criminal was reared among malefactors mitigates his fault in our eyes. The self-sacrifice of a father or mother, or self-sacrifice with the possibility of a reward, is more comprehensible than gratuitous self-sacrifice, and therefore seems less deserving of sympathy and less the result of free will. The founder of a sect or party, or an inventor, impresses us less when we know how or by what the way was prepared for his activity. If we have a large range of examples, if our observation is constantly directed to seeking the correlation of cause and effect in people's actions, their actions appear to us more under compulsion and less free the more correctly we connect the effects with the causes. If we examined simple actions and had a vast number of such actions under observation, our conception of their inevitability would be still greater. The dishonest conduct of the son of a dishonest father, the misconduct of a woman who had fallen into bad company, a drunkard's relapse into drunkenness, and so on are actions that seem to us less free the better we understand their cause. If the man whose actions we are considering is on a very low stage of mental development, like a child, a madman, or a simpleton—then, knowing the causes of the act and the simplicity of the character and intelligence in question, we see so large an element of necessity and so little free will that as soon as we know the cause prompting the action we can foretell the result.

On these three considerations alone is based the conception of irresponsibility for crimes and the extenuating circumstances admitted by all legislative codes. The responsibility appears greater or less according to our greater or lesser knowledge of the circumstances in which the man was placed whose action is being judged, and according to the greater or lesser interval of time between the commission of the action and its investigation, and according to the greater or lesser understanding of the causes that led to the action.

CHAPTER X

Thus our conception of free will and inevitability gradually diminishes or increases according to the greater or lesser connection with the external world, the greater or lesser remoteness of time, and the greater or lesser dependence on the causes in relation to which we contemplate a man's life.

So that if we examine the case of a man whose connection with the external world is well known, where the time between the action and its examination is great, and where the causes of the action are most accessible, we get the conception of a maximum of inevitability and a minimum of free will. If we examine a man little dependent on external conditions, whose action was performed very recently, and the causes of whose action are beyond our ken, we get the conception of a minimum of inevitability and a maximum of freedom.

In neither case—however we may change our point of view, however plain we may make to ourselves the connection between the man and the external world, however inaccessible it may be to us, however long or short the period of time, however intelligible or incomprehensible the causes of the action may be—can we ever conceive either complete freedom or complete necessity.

(1) To whatever degree we may imagine a man to be exempt from the influence of the external world, we never get a conception of freedom in space. Every human action is inevitably conditioned by what surrounds him and by his own body. I lift my arm and let it fall. My action seems to me free; but asking myself whether I could raise my arm in every direction, I see that I raised it in the direction in which there was least obstruction to that action either from things around me or from the construction of my own body. I chose one out of all the possible directions because in it there were fewest obstacles.

For my action to be free it was necessary that it should encounter no obstacles. To conceive of a man being free we must imagine him outside space, which is evidently impossible.

(2) However much we approximate the time of judgment to the time of the deed, we never get a conception of freedom in time. For if I examine an action committed a second ago I must still recognize it as not being free, for it is irrevocably linked to the moment at which it was committed. Can I lift my arm? I lift it, but ask myself: could I have abstained from lifting my arm at the moment that has already passed? To convince myself of this I do not lift it the next moment. But I am not now abstaining from doing so at the first moment when I asked the question. Time has gone by which I could not detain, the arm I then lifted is no longer the same as the arm I now refrain from lifting, nor is the air in which I lifted it the same that now surrounds me. The moment in which the first movement was made is irrevocable, and at that moment I could make only one movement, and whatever movement I made would be the only one. That I did not lift my arm a moment later does not prove that I could have abstained from lifting it then. And since I could make only one movement at that single moment of time, it could not have been any other. To imagine it as free, it is necessary to imagine it in the present, on the boundary between the past and the future—that is, outside time, which is impossible.

(3) However much the difficulty of understanding the causes may be increased, we never reach a conception of complete freedom, that is, an absence of cause. However inaccessible to us may be the cause of the expression of will in any action, our own or another's, the first demand of reason is the assumption of and search for a cause, for without a cause no phenomenon is conceivable. I raise my arm to perform an action independently of any cause, but my wish to perform an action without a cause is the cause of my action.

But even if—imagining a man quite exempt from all influences, examining only his momentary action in the present, unevoked by any cause—we were to admit so infinitely small a remainder of inevitability as equaled zero, we should even then not have arrived at the conception of complete freedom in man, for a being uninfluenced by the external world, standing outside of time and independent of cause, is no longer a man.

In the same way we can never imagine the action of a man quite devoid of freedom and entirely subject to the law of inevitability.

(1) However we may increase our knowledge of the conditions of space in which man is situated, that knowledge can never be complete, for the number of those conditions is as infinite as the infinity of space. And therefore so long as not *all* the conditions influencing men are defined, there is no complete inevitability but a certain measure of freedom remains.

(2) However we may prolong the period of time between the action we are examining and the judgment upon it, that period will be finite, while time is infinite, and so in this respect too there can never be absolute inevitability.

(3) However accessible may be the chain of causation of any action, we shall never know the whole chain since it is endless, and so again we never reach absolute inevitability.

But besides this, even if, admitting the remaining minimum of freedom to equal zero, we assumed in some given case—as for instance in that of a dying man, an unborn babe, or an idiot—complete absence of freedom, by so doing we should destroy the very conception of man in the case we are examining, for as soon as there is no freedom there is also no man. And so the conception of the action of a man subject solely to the law of inevitability without any element of freedom is just as impossible as the conception of a man's completely free action.

And so to imagine the action of a man entirely subject to the law of inevitability without any freedom, we must assume the knowledge of an *infinite* number of space relations, an *infinitely* long period of time, and an *infinite* series of causes.

To imagine a man perfectly free and not subject to the law of inevitability, we must imagine him all alone, *beyond space, beyond time,* and *free from dependence on cause.*

In the first case, if inevitability were possible without freedom we should have reached a definition of inevitability by the laws of inevitability itself, that is, a mere form without content.

In the second case, if freedom were possible without inevitability we should have arrived at unconditioned freedom beyond space, time, and cause, which by the fact of its being unconditioned and unlimited would be nothing, or mere content without form.

We should in fact have reached those two fundamentals of which man's whole outlook on the universe is constructed—the incomprehensible essence of life, and the laws defining that essence.

Reason says: (1) space with all the forms of matter that give it visibility is infinite, and cannot be imagined otherwise. (2) Time is infinite motion without a moment of rest and is unthinkable otherwise. (3) The connection between cause and effect has no beginning and can have no end.

Consciousness says: (1) I alone am, and all that exists is but me, consequently I include space. (2) I measure flowing time by the fixed moment of the present in which alone I am conscious of myself as living, consequently I am outside time. (3) I am beyond cause, for I feel myself to be the cause of every manifestation of my life.

Reason gives expression to the laws of inevitability. Consciousness gives expression to the essence of freedom.

Freedom not limited by anything is the essence of life, in man's consciousness. Inevitability without content is man's reason in its three forms.

Freedom is the thing examined. Inevitability is what examines. Freedom is the content. Inevitability is the form.

Only by separating the two sources of cognition, related to one another as form to content, do we get the mutually exclusive and separately incomprehensible conceptions of freedom and inevitability.

Only by uniting them do we get a clear conception of man's life.

Apart from these two concepts which in their union mutually define one another as form and content, no conception of life is possible.

All that we know of the life of man is merely a certain relation of free will to inevitability, that is, of consciousness to the laws of reason.

All that we know of the external world of nature is only a certain relation of the forces of nature to inevitability, or of the essence of life to the laws of reason.

The great natural forces lie outside us and we are not conscious of them; we call those forces gravitation, inertia, electricity, animal force, and so on, but we are conscious of the force of life in man and we call that freedom.

But just as the force of gravitation, incomprehensible in itself but felt by every man, is understood by us only to the extent to which we know the laws of inevitability to which it is subject (from the first knowledge that all bodies have weight, up to Newton's law), so too the force of free will, incomprehensible in itself but of which everyone is conscious, is intelligible to us only in as far as we know the laws of inevitability to which it is subject (from the fact that every man dies, up to the knowledge of the most complex economic and historic laws).

All knowledge is merely a bringing of this essence of life under the laws of reason.

Man's free will differs from every other force in that man is directly conscious of it, but in the eyes of reason it in no way differs from any other force. The forces of gravitation, electricity, or chemical affinity are only distinguished from one another in that they are differently defined by reason. Just so the force of man's free will is distinguished by reason from the other forces of nature only by the definition reason gives it. Freedom, apart from necessity, that is, apart from the laws of reason that define it, differs in no way from gravitation, or heat, or the force that makes things grow; for reason, it is only a momentary undefinable sensation of life.

And as the undefinable essence of the force moving the heavenly bodies, the undefinable essence of the forces of heat and electricity, or of chemical affinity, or of the vital force, forms the content of astronomy, physics, chemistry, botany, zoology, and so on, just in the same way does the force of free will form the content of history. But just as the subject of every science is the manifestation of this unknown essence of life while that essence itself can only be the subject of metaphysics, even the manifestation of the force of free will in human beings in space, in time, and in dependence on cause forms the subject of history, while free will itself is the subject of metaphysics.

In the experimental sciences what we know we call the laws of inevitability, what is unknown to us we call vital force. Vital force is only an expression for the unknown remainder over and above what we know of the essence of life.

So also in history what is known to us we call laws of inevitability, what is unknown we call free will. Free will is for history only an expression for the unknown remainder of what we know about the laws of human life.

CHAPTER XI

History examines the manifestations of man's free will in connection with the external world in time and in dependence on cause, that is, it defines this freedom by the laws of reason, and so history is a science only in so far as this free will is defined by those laws.

The recognition of man's free will as something capable of influencing historical events, that is, as not subject to laws, is the same for history as the recognition of a free force moving the heavenly bodies would be for astronomy.

That assumption would destroy the possibility of the existence of laws, that is, of any science whatever. If there is even a single body moving freely, then the laws of Kepler and Newton are negatived and no conception of the movement of the heavenly bodies any longer exists. If any single action is due to free will, then not a single historical law can exist, nor any conception of historical events.

For history, lines exist of the movement of human wills, one end of which is hidden in the unknown but at the other end of which a consciousness of man's will in the present moves in space, time, and dependence on cause.

The more this field of motion spreads out before our eyes, the more evident are the laws of that movement. To discover and define those laws is the problem of history.

From the standpoint from which the science of history now regards its subject on the path it now follows, seeking the causes of events in man's free will, a scientific enunciation of those laws is impossible, for however man's free will may be restricted, as soon as we recognize it as a force not subject to law, the existence of law becomes impossible.

Only by reducing this element of free will to the infinitesimal, that is, by regarding it as an infinitely small quantity, can we convince ourselves of the absolute inaccessibility of the causes, and then instead of seeking causes, history will take the discovery of laws as its problem.

The search for these laws has long been begun and the new methods of thought which history must adopt are being worked out simultaneously with the self-destruction toward which—ever dissecting and dissecting the causes of phenomena—the old method of history is moving.

All human sciences have traveled along that path. Arriving at infinitesimals, mathematics, the most exact of sciences, abandons the process of analysis and enters on the new process of the integration of unknown, infinitely small, quantities. Abandoning the conception of cause, mathematics seeks law, that is, the property common to all unknown, infinitely small, elements.

In another form but along the same path of reflection the other sciences have proceeded. When Newton enunciated the law of gravity he did not say that the sun or the earth had a property of attraction; he said that all bodies from the largest to the smallest have the property of attracting one another, that is, leaving aside the question of the cause of the movement of the bodies, he expressed the property common to all bodies from the infinitely large to the infinitely small. The same is done by the natural sciences: leaving aside the question of cause, they seek for laws. History stands on the same path. And if history has for its object the study of the movement of the nations and of humanity and not the narration of episodes in the lives of individuals, it too, setting aside the conception of cause, should seek the laws common to all the inseparably interconnected infinitesimal elements of free will.

CHAPTER XII

From the time the law of Copernicus was discovered and proved, the mere recognition of the fact that it was not the sun but the earth that moves sufficed to destroy the whole cosmography of the ancients. By disproving that law it might have been possible to retain the old conception of the movements of the bodies, but without disproving it, it would seem impossible to continue studying the Ptolemaic worlds. But even after the discovery of the law of Copernicus the Ptolemaic worlds were still studied for a long time.

From the time the first person said and proved that the number of births or of crimes is subject to mathematical laws, and that this or that mode of government is determined by certain geographical and economic conditions, and that certain relations of population to soil produce migrations of peoples, the foundations on which history had been built were destroyed in their essence.

By refuting these new laws the former view of history might have been retained; but without refuting them it would seem impossible to continue studying historic events as the results of man's free will. For if a certain mode of government was established or certain migrations of peoples took place in consequence of such and such geographic, ethnographic, or economic conditions, then the free will of those individuals who appear to us to have established that mode of government or occasioned the migrations can no longer be regarded as the cause.

And yet the former history continues to be studied side by side with the laws of statistics, geography, political economy, comparative philology, and geology, which directly contradict its assumptions.

The struggle between the old views and the new was long and stubbornly fought out in physical philosophy. Theology stood on guard for the old views and accused the new of violating revelation. But when truth conquered, theology established itself just as firmly on the new foundation.

Just as prolonged and stubborn is the struggle now proceeding between the old and the new conception of history, and theology in the same way stands on guard for the old view, and accuses the new view of subverting revelation.

In the one case as in the other, on both sides the struggle provokes passion and stifles truth. On the one hand there is fear and regret for the loss of the whole edifice constructed through the ages, on the other is the passion for destruction.

To the men who fought against the rising truths of physical philosophy, it seemed that if they admitted that truth it would destroy faith in God, in the creation of the firmament, and in the miracle of Joshua the son of Nun. To the defenders of the laws of Copernicus and Newton, to Voltaire for example, it seemed that the laws of astronomy destroyed religion, and he utilized the law of gravitation as a weapon against religion.

Just so it now seems as if we have only to admit the law of inevitability, to destroy the conception of the soul, of good and evil, and all the institutions of state and church that have been built up on those conceptions.

So too, like Voltaire in his time, uninvited defenders of the law of inevitability today use that law as a weapon against religion, though the law of inevitability in history, like the law of Copernicus in astronomy, far from destroying, even strengthens the foundation on which the institutions of state and church are erected.

As in the question of astronomy then, so in the question of history now, the whole difference of opinion is based on the recognition or nonrecognition of something absolute, serving as the measure of visible phenomena. In astronomy it was the immovability of the earth, in history it is the independence of personality—free will.

As with astronomy the difficulty of recognizing the motion of the earth lay in abandoning the immediate sensation of the earth's fixity and of the motion of the planets, so in history the difficulty of recognizing the subjection of personality to the laws of space, time, and cause lies in renouncing the direct feeling of the independence of one's own personality. But as in astronomy the new view said: "It is true that we do not feel the movement of the earth, but by admitting its immobility we arrive at absurdity, while by admitting its motion (which we do not feel) we arrive at laws," so also in history the new view says: "It is true that we are not conscious of our dependence, but by admitting our free will we arrive at absurdity, while by admitting our dependence on the external world, on time, and on cause, we arrive at laws."

In the first case it was necessary to renounce the consciousness of an unreal immobility in space and to recognize a motion we did not feel; in the present case it is similarly necessary to renounce a freedom that does not exist, and to recognize a dependence of which we are not conscious.